MW00764394

At the end of the day,
as the sun starts to set,
as the moon makes
its way to the sky.

As the dark inky shadows stretch out like a cat,
poor Pup, he lets out a sigh.

5

He tries counting
sheep and gives them
all names, until he can
think of no more.

6

He counts all the stars that light up the sky,
but nothing will help little Pup snore.

He chases his tail and chews on a bone.

He plays with the mice in the hall.

He rolls like a hedgehog and howls at the moon,
but poor Pup cannot rest at all.

The night shift begins for the beetles and bugs,
as they march from their beds by the log.

The moths and
the fireflies
dance through
the night
and sing
"go to sleep, little dog!"

Hopelessly he tries to slip into sleep,
to drift into magical dreams.

12

He patrols with the fox through whispering grass, lit up by the moon's silver beams.

13

He skips with the **dragonflies** down to
the **pond**, and tickles the fish with his toes.

He floats on the lilies and leaps with the frogs, and ripples the pond with his nose.

As stars paint their light
all over the land, little Pup
looks up at their glow.

16

As badger
peeps out
from a carpet
of leaves,
he whispers
"to bed you must go."

Nothing he tries brings sleep to his eyes,
nothing will make Pup yawn.

So with a **THUD**
of a paw, he plods across
the floor and returns
to his basket forlorn.

19

As the clock strikes
eleven, Mommy
returns, to kiss
and cuddle Pup tight.

20

With a special new blanket, she wraps up her pup
and quietly turns off the light.

The magical blanket so soft and so warm,
is like the loveliest, fluffiest sheep.

It covers little Pup in the happiest warmth
and at last he falls fast asleep.

24

# There's Only One
# Scruffle

## Robert Dunn

Ellie loved Scruffle.
He was her bear, and that was that.

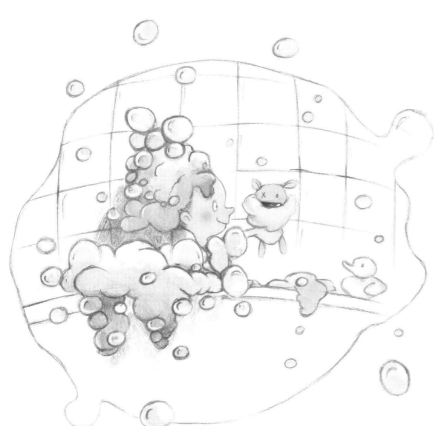

Ellie and Scruffle did everything together.

In fact, they were **inseparable.**

Ellie's mom and dad didn't understand
why she loved Scruffle so much.

He only had one eye, was
held together with moldy old thread...

...and had a very curious smell.

He smelled a bit like stale cheese
and old socks. **Yuck!**

Ellie's mom decided that she should have
a new bear—one with two eyes, clean
thread, and that smelled of strawberries.

Ellie didn't like the new bear. He smelled **wrong!**

"Can I keep him in the garbage can?" Ellie asked.

"No, you most certainly cannot!" replied Mom.

"You could try playing with him, for a little while at least," Mom said.

"You won't know what he's really like until you've spent a little time together."

So Ellie thought about it, then decided
to take a walk and think about it some more.

She thought about it while she
played cowboys with Teabag.

Thump!

Thump!

Thump!

34

helped Grandpa in the garden...

COMPOST

37

...and she thought about it while
she painted a picture for Scruffle.

38

Ellie eventually decided that she would play with the new bear. However, he didn't smell quite as fresh as he had in the morning.

In fact, he smelled **DISGUSTING!**

"Well, I couldn't possibly play with him now!" said Ellie, triumphant.

"Why do you love
Scruffle so much?"
Mom sighed.

Ellie handed Scruffle to her mom. "Well, you
won't know what he's really like until you've
spent a little time together, will you?" she smiled.

Ellie's mom suddenly noticed how
soft and cuddly Scruffle was,
if you ignored the smell!

Ellie knew her mom finally understood.
Scruffle was Ellie's bear and that was enough for Mom.

"Can I keep Scruffle and
the new bear?" Ellie asked.

"Of course," said Mom, "but after they've both gone through the washing machine!"

45

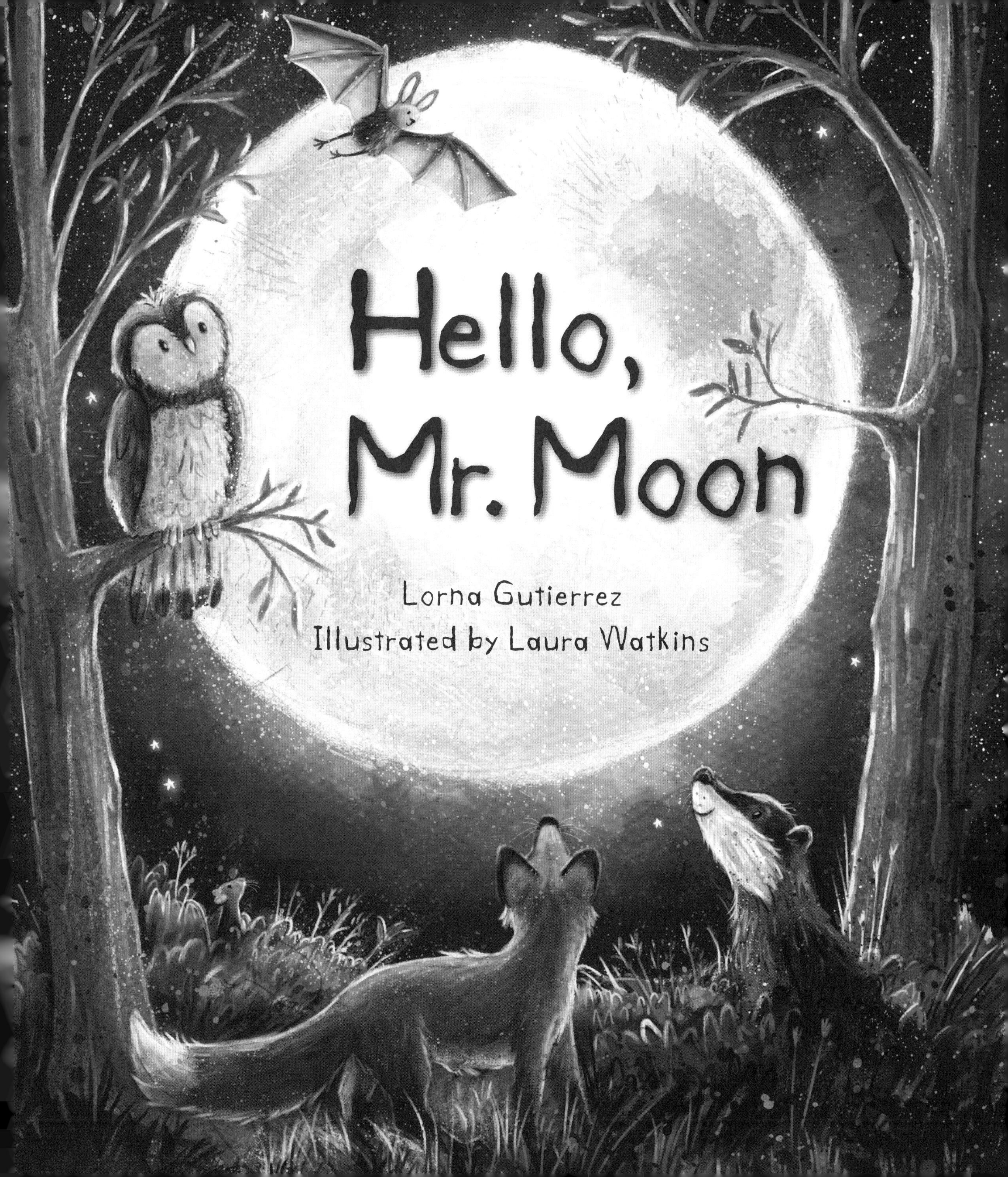

# Hello, Mr. Moon

Lorna Gutierrez

Illustrated by Laura Watkins

Hello, Mr. Moon.
You're looking full today,
unlike before, when you
were wasting away.

Are you taking
care of yourself?
You're **up.** You're **down.**
Why so skinny
and then so round?

Relax, little child. You will see, things happen that make me – ME!

It takes one year for Earth to get around the Sun –
365 days and its job is done!

Once a month I orbit, too –
but not around the Sun, just around you.

I'm lit by the Sun, that's why I seem bright –
you're seeing my sunlit side at night.

The movement of Earth, Sun, and me
causes different phases... that's what you see!

But sometimes you're not there. Where'd you go? You disappear!

Sunlight is behind me – it's called my new moon.
It means you can't see me, but you will soon!

I must admit, I enjoy less light –
it's easier for me to sneak around at night!

A sliver of light shows
my crescent moon lit.
The sunlight on me
is only a bit.

Half bright, Mr. Moon is something to see.
You're black and white – just like me!

That's my quarter moon, though some call it half.

See how I change as I follow my path?

Close to full, you shimmer
and shine, reflecting on my ocean
in a way that's so fine.

Now I'm gibbous, nearly all bright.
See my glimmer on your waters tonight.

Your light is so peaceful, it's really quite nice...

...shining brightly as I look for mice.

Full is my glory:
all eyes are on me!
I'm completely
lit and easy to see.

I like to play and heard you do, too.
What, exactly, do you do?

Yes, little cat, I do have some tricks –
like my brilliant, red, lunar eclipse.

Thanks, Mr. Moon, we know you care,
even if we can't see you, you're still there!

New Moon

Crescent Moon

Quarter Moon

64

Gibbous Moon

Full Moon

Yes my friends, although I seem far,
I'll follow you, wherever you are.

Now nighttime is over
and it's almost day.
It's time for other animals
to come out and play.

But remember, just
look **UP**, and I'll look **down,**
and know that I'll always
be around.

67

# Shark's Big Surprise

A. H. Benjamin and Bill Bolton

Shark had sharp, pointy teeth.
He looked scary. Everyone hid from him.

"It's not fair,"
he thought sadly.

"No one wants
to play
with me."

70

One day, Shark had an idea. The idea kept
him busy all day. When he was ready, he left
the old, sunken ship where he lived. . .

71

Shark lurked behind a large rock.
Soon Octopus came along, his
long arms
splish-splashing.

Shark **pounced.**

"**Got you!**"
he snapped.

And he put Octopus in a large bag.

"**Help!**" wailed Octopus.

Shark swam off.

73

Shark hid inside the thick seaweed.

Soon Lobster appeared, her sharp pincers **click-clacking.**

74

Shark **pounced.**

"**Got you!**" he snapped.
And he put Lobster in the bag.

"**Oh, no!**" cried Lobster.
Shark set off **again...**

75

Shark slid into a dark cave, and waited.

Before long, Turtle paddled by, his large flippers flip-flapping.

Shark **pounced.**

Shark **pounced** once more.

Soon Starfish was
in Shark's bag.

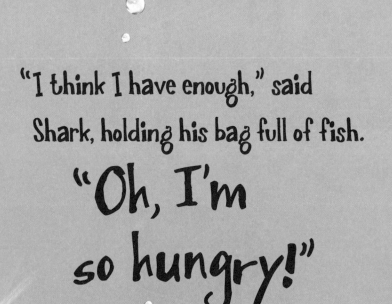

"I think I have enough," said Shark, holding his bag full of fish.

"**Oh, I'm so hungry!**"

he said, setting off for home.

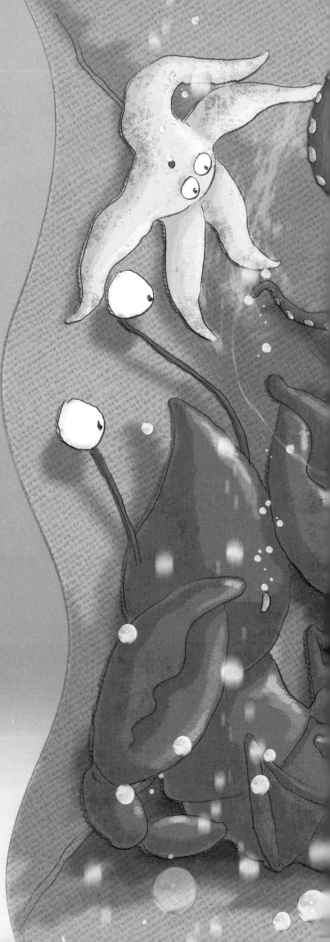

82

"Shark's going to eat us all for lunch!" Jellyfish cried.

But what could they do?

83

Soon Shark was back at home.
"I'm so pleased," he said,
as he emptied his bag.

84

Everyone was terrified as they tumbled out.

"It's the end of us!"
Lobster wailed.

Suddenly Shark turned around and said... 85

**"SURPRISE!** I made it myself...

...and I wondered if you would like to share it with me!"

"You gave us quite a scare," said Octopus. "Next time you want us to join you for cake, you could just ask..."

# BATMOUSE

### Steve Smallman

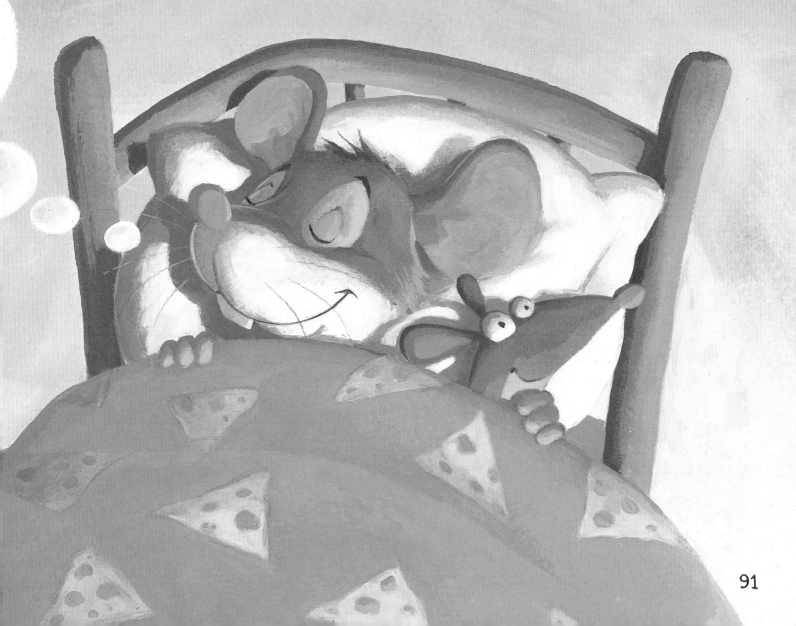

# squeeeeeeak!

"Look, Mom," said Pip.
"It's a flying mouse!"

"That's not a mouse,"
said Mom. "It's a bat."

"I wish I could fly," said Pip.
"When I grow up, can I be a bat?"

"You can't be a bat," said Mom.
"Look—you don't have any wings."

So Pip made some wings out of an
old cardboard box. Soon he was
ready for takeoff!

# "Look, Mom. I'm a batmouse!"

Pip rushed around, squeaking his squeakiest
squeak and flapping his cardboard wings up
and down. But he just couldn't fly.

So he tried again . . .

. . . and again . . .

. . . and again!

He flapped till he flopped,
tired and dizzy on the floor.

"Never mind, Pip," said Mom.
To cheer him up, she made his favorite meal:
stinky cheese and cracker crumbs.

At bedtime, Pip couldn't get comfortable.
His wings kept getting caught in the blanket.

"That's because bats
hang upside down
when they sleep,"
said Mom.

Pip tried lying upside down.
But he still wasn't comfortable.

The next morning, Pip climbed
up to the top of Windy Hill.

"Time to fly!" he squeaked,
flapping his wings as hard as
he could. Pip jumped!

BUMP!

He landed on his bottom
and rolled, over and
over and over, all the
way down the hill.

Pip's head was spinning,
his bottom was bruised, and his
wings were all tattered and torn.

Then he heard a familiar sound . . .

Squeeeeeeak!

It was coming from inside a little cave.
The cave was dark and spooky,
but Pip tried to be brave.

"H...h...hello?"

he squeaked.

"Hello," said an
upside-down voice.
"I'm Albert. Who are you?"

"I'm P . . . P . . . P . . . Pip,
and **I'm a batmouse!**"

"Really?" asked Albert.
"But you seem to be
the wrong way up."

"Oops, sorry!" said Pip,
and he stood on his head.

103

"Your wings look a little . . . cardboardy,"
said Albert.

"My real wings haven't
grown yet!" said Pip.

"Ah, that explains it," said Albert with a smile.
"Well, little batmouse, are you hungry?"
Pip was VERY hungry.

104

"Do you have any stinky cheese?" he asked.

"Stinky cheese!" cried Albert. "Bats don't eat stinky cheese! How about a nice, juicy moth?"

Pip looked at the moth
and burst into tears.

"I'M NOT A
BATMOUSE!"

he blurted.

106

"I DON'T WANT TO
LIVE IN A SPOOKY CAVE,

OR EAT MOFFS,

OR HANG UPSIDE DOWN . . .

. . . BUT I REALLY, REALLY WANT TO FLY!"

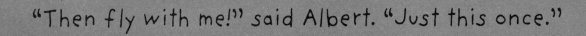

"Then fly with me!" said Albert. "Just this once."

He picked up Pip and carried him
out into the twinkly, twilight sky.

They soared over Windy Hill, through the treetops,

and finally landed right outside of Pip's house.

"Well, little batmouse," whispered
Albert, "do you like flying?"

"I think so," said Pip, who felt dizzy and scared
and excited all at once. "Thank you, Albert."

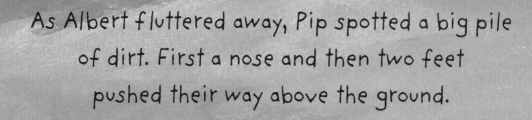

As Albert fluttered away, Pip spotted a big pile
of dirt. First a nose and then two feet
pushed their way above the ground.

"LOOK MOM!"
Pip cried.
"It's a DIGGING MOUSE!"

"That's not a mouse, Pip. It's a mole," said Mom.
"When I grow up, can I be a mole?" asked Pip.

"Here we go again . . ." sighed Mom.

112

# The Star of the Zoo

Virginie Zurcher

Daniel Howarth

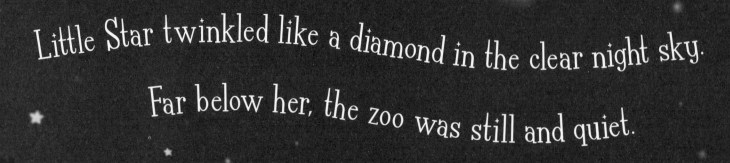

Little Star twinkled like a diamond in the clear night sky.
Far below her, the zoo was still and quiet.

The animals were getting ready for bed.

Then suddenly . . . .

115

Little
Star
lost
her
balance
and
tumbled
out
of the
sky!

Lion could lift up
Little Star easily, but he
couldn't reach the sky.

"I can help!"
called Ant.

"Rahahaha," laughed
Lion. "You're too small.
You can't help."

121

"I'll help you," said Monkey. "I'm the best climber in the zoo."

Monkey picked up Little Star and jumped into a tree. He swung through the branches to the very top.

Monkey climbed as high as he could, but he couldn't reach the sky.

"I have a plan!" called Ant.

"Hoohoohaha," laughed Monkey. "You're too small. You can't help."

123

"I'll help you," said Giraffe.
"I'm the tallest animal
in the zoo."

Giraffe picked up Little
Star, stood up straight,
and stretched her neck
as far as she could.

Giraffe was very tall, but she couldn't reach the sky.

"I know what to do!" called Ant.

"Heeheehee," laughed Giraffe. "You're too small. You can't help."

Little Star's
brightness
was fading.

"I have to be back in
the sky before sunrise,"
she cried.

"Give me a chance–I can help!" called Ant.

The animals all just stared at Ant. What could she do?

"Well, if you think you
can do it, you might as
well try," said Lion,
rolling his eyes.

128

Ant scuttled off . . . .

129

She came back, not with
ten, not with a hundred,
but with thousands
of friends to help.

Ant picked up Little Star
and climbed onto another
ant's back.

That ant climbed
onto another ant.

And that ant climbed
onto another.

The
tower
of
ants
grew
higher
and
higher
until . . .

. . . they reached the sky!

131

"You did it!"
shouted Little Star.

All of the animals cheered.

"Anything's possible
if you work together!"
Ant said proudly.

Little Chick's family were all fast asleep. But Little Chick wasn't.

She peeked out of the peephole and saw a big silvery moon shining on the river.

135

She followed the moonlight to the end of the river, where it danced out over the sea.

Little Chick hopped into a boat. "Maybe I can sleep here," she thought.

But when Little Chick tried to sleep, she just couldn't. The waves were too noisy, the wind was too cold.

"Oh, what's the secret
of sleep?" she peeped.
"Follow me," said the Moon,
"and I'll show you."

Over the water went Little Chick,
till she came to Monkey Island.

"What's the secret of sleep?"
she asked a lonely monkey.

"It's so boring here
alone," said Monkey.
"I never get tired
enough to sleep."

141

So, Little Chick
raced Monkey...

...and Monkey
chased
Little Chick.

Soon, Monkey was soundly snoozing.
"So you have to be tired to sleep!" peeped Little Chick.
"Yes," said the Moon. "But that's not all!"

Monkey and Little Chick sailed away to the Island of Fire.

"Hello," said Little Chick to a baby dragon.
"Do you know any secrets of sleep?"
"No, I can't sleep either. I'm too scared of
big DRAGON MONSTERS!" said Dragon.

Little Chick sang Dragon one of her mama's cluck-a-byes till he was deeply dozing.

"So you have to be tired and you have to feel safe?" she said. "Yes," said the Moon, "but sometimes even that's not enough..."

The boat set sail to the Land of Icicles.
The wind was sharp, the sky was frozen,
and poor Little Chick was all shivery-shaky.

So the baby dragon puffed warm air all around her
till she was warm as toast—and sleepy, too.

"Oh, you have to be as cozy as cozy can be," said Little Chick.

They sailed a long way away,
and Little Chick's eyes began to close.
But not for long—for there, on Mighty Island,
was a herd of noisy elephants.
"Ta-rum! Ta-raa!" they sang.

"They trumpet all night," moaned a
tired little elephant. "I can never sleep."
"Ah!" said Little Chick. "So it has to be quiet!
Well, I know a place that's quiet at night…"

So she sailed away with her three new friends.

"You're back, Little Chick!" clucked Mama and Papa.
"Yes, and I think I can sleep now…" yawned Little Chick.

For at last
she'd found all of
the secrets of sleep.
You need to be:

tired, safe, cozy, and quiet.

# The Not-so-Perfect Penguin

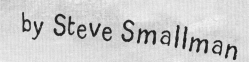

by Steve Smallman

On a snowy, blowy island in the middle of the sea lived a group of perfect penguins. They were **smart** and **serious** and **sensible**.

All except for Percy, who was...

well...

not so perfect.

The other penguins ate their dinners sensibly.
But Percy always played with his food.

"Eat nicely, Percy!"
the biggest penguin said.

While the other penguins **waddled** along seriously, Percy **slid** on his tummy.

"Be careful, Percy," the oldest penguin grumbled.

The other penguins swam smoothly through the water, catching lots of fish. But Percy liked to jump and play, doing somersaults and landing with a big...

SPLASH!

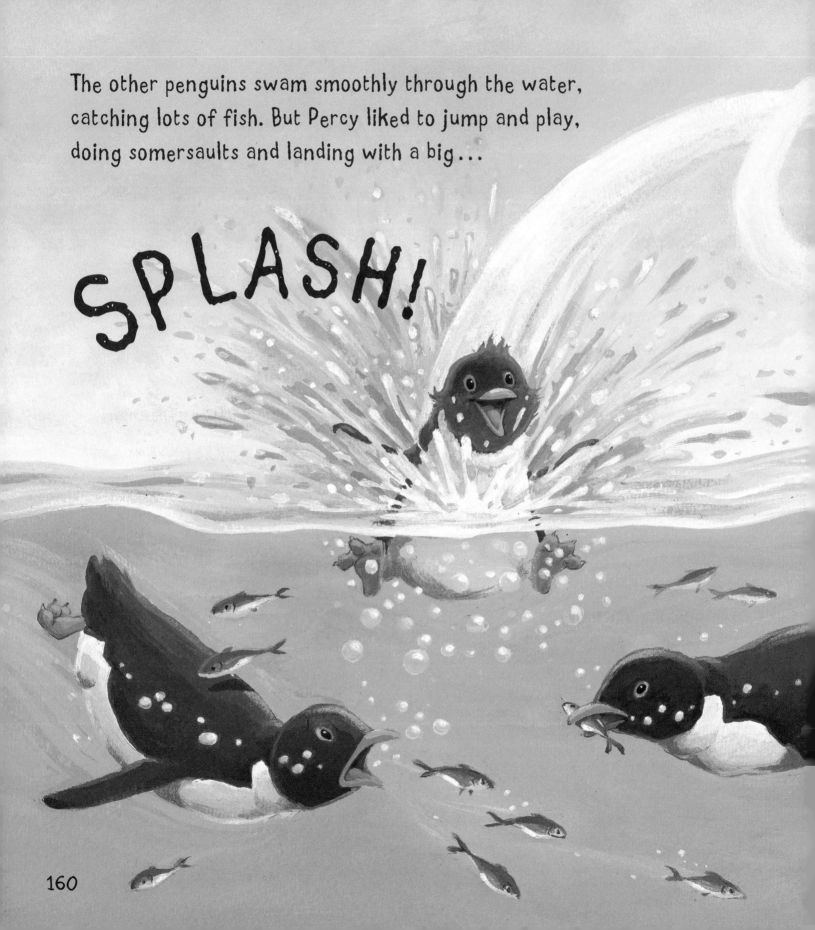

"Look out, Percy," the smallest penguin said. "You silly penguin!"

When it was really cold, all the penguins huddled together. Percy felt **warm** and **safe** in the middle of the group.

But then, **oh dear**, he needed to...

FAAAAAAAART!

164

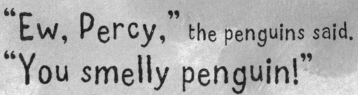

"Ew, Percy," the penguins said.
"You smelly penguin!"

They went and stood away from Percy.

165

Percy waddled away sadly.
"My friends think I'm **silly** and **smelly**.
I'll never be **perfect** like them..."

The snow fell harder and the wind blew stronger.
"It's cold on my own," said Percy, shivering.

Percy made himself a new friend from snow and ice,
but the snow penguin wasn't very warm to cuddle with.

167

Without Percy, the penguins ate their dinners sensibly.

**"It's so quiet!"** the oldest penguin said.

They swam seriously, without splashing.

**"It's rather dull!"** the biggest penguin said.

They waddled along
in a straight line.

"It's a bit boring!"
the fluffiest penguin said.

"I wish Percy
were here," the
smallest penguin said.

"What will happen to Percy?" the oldest penguin said.
"He's all alone in the freezing cold." The penguins began to worry.

So they waddled off through the swirling snow to look for Percy.

170

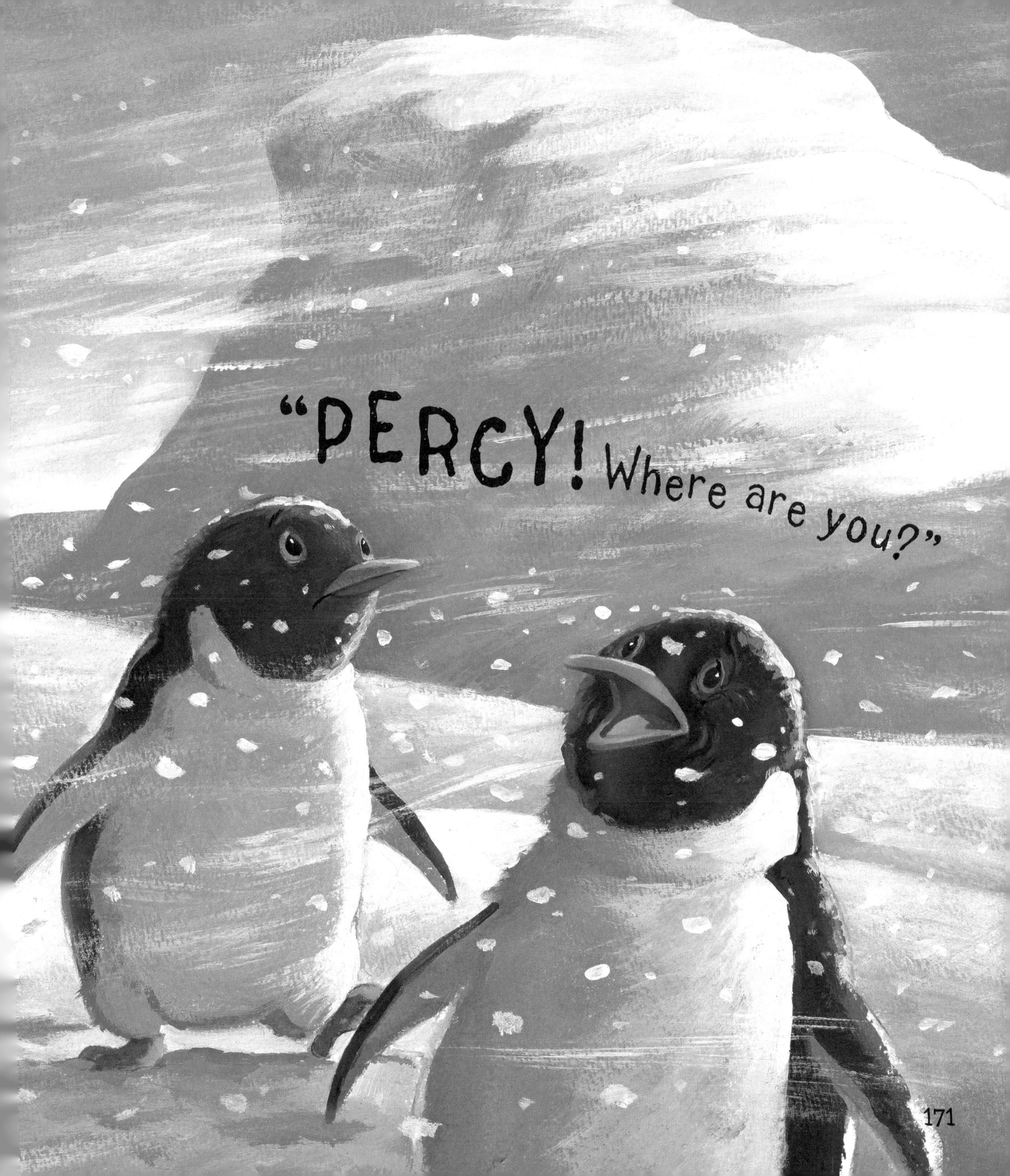

"PERCY! Where are you?"

In an icy cave, they found two snow penguins.
One had lost its beak, but the other looked familiar.

It was Percy!

All the penguins gathered around and cuddled him.
Slowly, slowly, the snow began to melt.

Drip...

drip...

drip.

When Percy's flippers were free of snow,
he stretched and then...

TICKLE...

TICKLE...

TICKLE!

The penguins all fell down laughing.

"Oh Percy," the smallest penguin giggled.
"It's good to have you back!"

Surrounded by happy penguins, Percy felt that
maybe he didn't need to be perfect after all.
His friends loved him just as he was.

# Goodbye for now!